Welcome to Planet Reader!

Invite your child on a journey to a wonderful, imaginative place—the limitless universe of reading! And there's no better traveling companion than you, the parent. Every time you and your child read together you send out an important message: Reading can be rewarding and *fun*. This understanding is essential to helping your child build the skills and confidence he or she needs as an emerging reader.

Here are some tips for sharing Planet Reader stories with your child:

Be open! Some children like to listen to or read the whole story and then ask questions. Some children will stop on every page with a question or a comment. Either way is fine; the most important thing is that your child feels reading is a pleasurable experience.

Be understanding! Sometimes your child might need a direct answer. If he or she points to a word and asks you to tell what it is, do so. Other times, your child may want to sound out a word or stop to figure out a sentence independently. Allow for both approaches.

Enjoy! The story and characters in this book were created especially for your child's age group. Talk about the story. Take turns reading favorite parts. Look at how the illustrations support the story and enhance the reading experience.

And most of all, enjoy your child's journey into literacy. It's one of the most important trips the two of you will ever take!

*For Elizabeth Ensley,
a wonderful teacher and friend*

*With special thanks to
Linda Murray, Patsy Jensen,
and Dorit Radandt*

Ivy Green, Cootie Queen

by Joan Holub

Chapter 1

I Do Not Have Cooties!

Do book reports give you cooties? Mine almost did.
My name is Ivy Green, and this is the story of how
I became Cootie Queen of Snoozer Elementary School.
It all began with a book report. . . .

"Earth to Ivy Green," singsonged a
nearby voice.

I looked up. "Huh?"

Holly was leaning over her desk, waving
one hand back and forth in front of my
face. "I called you *three* times," she said.

"Where's Ms. Girth?" I asked, looking
around the classroom for our teacher.

"In the hall," Holly replied.

I pushed my open book toward her. "Isn't this cool?"

Holly frowned at the picture in my book. "What is it?"

"A bacteria that lives on eyelashes."

"Eyelash bugs? Yuk!" Holly cried, scrunching her nose. "Why are you reading *that?*"

"For my book report this Friday," I said. I studied the picture of the bacteria enlarged under a microscope. "You don't think this book is *too* gross, do you? I don't want to make the whole class start gagging or anything."

Suddenly I noticed someone standing right by my desk. Someone with tiny roses on her shirt. I knew without even looking up that it was Rose Thornton, the most popular girl in our class. Absolutely everything she wore had roses on it.

Rose leaned against my desk and stared at me like she thought I was weird. "There aren't any bugs on *my* skin," she told me in her snooty voice. *Oh no!* I thought. She must have heard me talking about my book.

"You'd better hope there are," I replied. "Otherwise your skin might rot and fall off."

Rose frowned. Her best friends, Violet and Lily, hurried over to see what was happening. Violet's shirt had violet flowers on it, and there were lily-shaped barrettes in Lily's long blonde hair. They had a club called the Flower Girls, and they always wore stuff with their flowers on it.

"Ivy is reading a book about cooties," Rose told her friends. "I guess she's trying to figure out how to get rid of hers."

Violet and Lily giggled as if that were the funniest thing they had ever heard.

"Who said anything about cooties?" I asked. "I was talking about bacteria."

"Same thing," said Rose. She twirled her necklace so that it wound and unwound around one finger.

"There's no such thing as cooties," I
insisted.

Two more kids scooted their chairs over
to listen. "What's happening?" they
wanted to know.

"Ivy's got cooties!" Rose informed them.

"I do not!" I cried. "You think *everybody* has cooties. I bet you don't even know what a cootie is."

"I sure know what one looks like," said Rose, poking a finger at my chest. "You are the *queen* of the cooties."

"Ivy Green—Cootie Queen!" shouted Violet. Rose and Lily almost fell over laughing.

"Ms. Girth is coming!" Holly yelled. Everyone zoomed back to their desks.

"I wish Rose would go back to ignoring me," I whispered to Holly.

I would wish it even more before the day ended.

Chapter 2

My Life Is Over

Holly and I were eating our lunches at a picnic table. Over on the playground, a bunch of kids were hanging around Rose, Violet, and Lily.

"Why does everybody think those Flower Girls are so perfect?" I grumbled.

"Because they *are* perfect," Holly said. "Cute clothes. Cute hair. Cute everything. Perfect!"

"Perfectly stupid," I grumped. "They have a club that doesn't do anything."

"Maybe we should start our own club," Holly suggested.

"What kind?" I asked.

Holly sighed and snitched a few of my chips. "I don't know. All the good club ideas are taken."

"I think it should be a club where we actually *do* something," I said. "We could build an ant farm or . . . "

Holly wrinkled her nose and made a cross with two fingers like she was keeping vampires away. "No science stuff," she said.

"How about karate?" I asked.

Holly looked a little more interested in that idea but then shook her head. "We do enough karate in our class on Tuesday nights. I don't want to do more of it in a club. What about a dog club?"

"We don't have dogs, remember? Anyway, I'm not going to be in a dog club. The Flower Girls would probably bark every time we walked by." I stuffed my lunch leftovers in my bag, and we headed for the trash bins.

"Maybe the problem is that we need more members. Two kids aren't really enough for a club," said Holly.

Just then I noticed that Brad, the cutest boy in school, was tossing his trash in the bin ahead of us. Holly and I both had major crushes on him.

Brad looked up and smiled at us. I thought Holly was going to faint.

"Why don't you call your club 'The Cootie Club'?" someone behind us suggested. I whirled around and bumped into Brad's best friend, Jay. How had he found out about the cooties?

"Hey!" Jay screeched. "Don't touch me." He held out his left palm and drew two invisible lines on it with his right index finger.

He said: "Line, Line . . . " Then he stabbed his palm twice as if adding periods. "Dot! Dot! Now I've got my cootie shot! Ha! Ha! Ha!"

Brad glanced back as they walked

away, and I thought he looked sorry for me.

Holly stared after them in disbelief. "Rose must be telling everybody that you have cooties!"

"Now the whole school will call me 'Cootie Queen,'" I wailed. "Even Brad thinks I'm a giant cootie farm. My life is over at this school. I'm never coming back!"

Chapter 3

The Underwear Idea

The next morning I sat in front of the bathroom mirror. My sister, Margo, rubbed frosted green eyeshadow under my eyes. Then she leaned back, looked me over, and added a bit more.

"There," she said finally.

I studied my face in the mirror. "Do you think it will fool Mom?" I asked.

Margo shrugged. "You look sick to me, but I think Mom has built-in radar that tells her the difference between real and fake sick."

She began smoothing purple eyeshadow

on her eyelids. "I still don't understand why you're letting those stuck-up Flower Girls make you play sick for the rest of the week," Margo said. "Book reports are a snap. What are you so worried about?"

"Only about a hundred things," I said. "Like that I might start spitting or that boogers might be hanging from my nose. Or that the Flower Girls will call me a cootie queen . . ."

"Hey, that reminds me," Margo interrupted, dashing into her room. I followed and plopped down beside her on the bed. She picked up a magazine and flipped it open.

"This article lists a bunch of helpful tips," she said. She slid her finger down a page, stopping near the bottom. "Here! Under 'Helpful Hints for Public Speaking' it says: 'Try to imagine that your audience is in their underwear.'"

I wiggled around so I could read the words. "How's that going to help?"

"If the kids are in their underwear, they'll look dumb. Then you won't be afraid of them," Margo said.

I wrinkled my nose. "It won't work. I'll bet Rose wears perfect underwear."

"Just trying to help," said Margo. "We'd better get going." She grabbed her backpack, and we headed downstairs.

In the kitchen, Mom was stuffing papers into her briefcase. Margo sat down and sloshed milk on a bowl of cereal.

I leaned against the refrigerator. "Mom, I feel crummy," I moaned.

Looking worried, she slid one hand onto my forehead, cupped my chin with her other hand, and stared hard at my face.

I did my best to look droopy.

"Nice try," Mom said, ruffling my bangs. "But you're going to school. Go upstairs and wash off that green gunk."

I frowned at Margo. She made fists on either side of her head by her ears. One finger popped up from each fist, and she wiggled the fingers above each ear. She was right. Mom *did* have radar.

But I wasn't ready to give up yet. "I *can't* go to school today," I whined.

"Why not?" asked Mom. "Is there a problem at school?"

I couldn't tell her that the other kids thought I had cooties. She'd probably talk to Ms. Girth about it. Then Ms. Girth would talk to the Flower Girls. I'd never live that down.

I sighed. "No. No problem."

"Well, if you can't give me a reason for staying home, I expect you to go to school," said Mom.

"Oh, all right," I grumbled.

I stomped back upstairs and washed away the green. I wondered if Mom really did have radar or if the glittery sparkles in the eyeshadow had tipped her off.

Either way, I was stuck going to school.

Chapter 4

I Am Doomed

That afternoon, Holly and I raced ahead of the other kids into the library.

"Help me find a new book for my report," I begged, after we had claimed places at our favorite table.

"Are you dumping the coot—I mean, the bacteria book?" asked Holly.

I nodded. "I'd rather eat worms than give my report on *that* book."

"Ick!" said Holly.

"Well, maybe worm cookies would be okay," I said, knowing Holly would freak out.

She did. "Eeew! Double ick!" Holly was so easy to gross out, it wasn't even funny.

"I need a skinny book," I told her. "This is Tuesday, so I only have three nights to read a new book."

"How about this one?" asked Holly, holding up a thin blue book.

"No way!" I said. "I'd be laughed out of school if I did a book report on a baby book."

"But *all* of the skinny books are baby books," she protested. "Besides, I just remembered something. Tonight we have karate class. That means you'll only have two nights to read a new book."

"And write my report," I groaned. "Maybe I'd better look for a baby book after all."

Holly nodded. "While you're looking, I'm going to do some snooping. Those Flower Girls are up to something."

I peeked over at the table where Rose, Violet, and Lily were sitting. Their heads were pressed together so that brown, black, and blonde hair blended. They were whispering.

Holly went to the water fountain by their table. She pretended to drink for a long time, but I knew she was really spying. A few minutes later, she was back.

"The Flower Girls *are* up to no good," Holly whispered. "They're going to . . . "

Too late! Rose was already standing beside our table.

I looked up at her, but she ignored me. Everyone in our class was watching and waiting to hear what she would say.

"I don't think Ivy has cooties anymore," she said loudly. "I think she has . . . *poison ivy!*"

"Poison ivy!" sang Violet. The Flower Girls started scratching like they had poison ivy. Some kids began copying them, giggling and scratching, too. When the librarian ran over to shush everyone, Holly and I ducked outside.

"Just when I thought things couldn't get any worse—they did," I moped, once we were out in the hall. "I didn't even have time to get a new book. What am I going to do now?"

"I've got an idea," said Holly. "Why don't you just give your report on a book you've already read?"

"All the books I've read are weird or boring—to anyone but me, that is."

Holly looked at me and smiled sadly. "Well, you'll think of something."

I shook my head and sighed. "Thanks," I said, "but let's face it—I'm doomed."

At the end of the day, Ms. Girth announced to the class, "Remember, book reports are due on Friday."

As if I could forget!

Chapter 5

To Ivy Green's
Family,
You're invited to
see Ivy die of
embarrassment
next Tuesday.

Chop! Chop!

That night, Holly and I went to the dojo for our karate lessons. We wore loose white karate suits, called gi's.

As we sat down to remove our shoes, I glanced from the white belt I was wearing to the one around Holly's waist. Hers was white, too, but there were little yellow patches sewn on both ends.

"You're so lucky to be a yellow belt," I told her.

"You'll be one, too, after you pass the test," said Holly.

"Yeah, that'll happen in about a

million years," I said. To pass the test, I'd have to perform a special karate dance in front of judges. It made me shiver just thinking about it.

At that moment, Mr. Leow, our karate instructor, walked in.

"Attention, everyone," he said in a soft voice. The room got quiet instantly.

It's important to show respect in karate, so he bowed to us and we bowed to him. Then we did warm-up exercises.

"Clear your mind," Mr. Leow told us. "Try not to think of anything except the karate we are getting ready to do."

During class, I practiced my kata—the karate dance I would have to perform someday to earn my yellow belt. I had practiced so much that I could do the kata in my sleep. If only I could sleepwalk through my yellow-belt test!

At the end of class, Mr. Leow handed me a card. It was an invitation for Mom, Dad, and Margo to watch me take my

yellow-belt test—next Tuesday!

"You are ready to perform your kata in front of judges," Mr. Leow said with a smile. "It is time you earned your yellow belt."

On the way home I had a horrible thought. Other families would come to watch their kids take the test on Tuesday, too. Everyone would see my kata!

I could hardly get to sleep that night. Now I had *two* things to worry about: my book report *and* my karate test!

Chapter 6

The All New _Not_ Improved Ivy Green Frozen Popsicle

Nightmare in Ms. Girth's Class

Before I knew it, the dreaded day arrived. Friday. Book report day. I hadn't found another book, so I was stuck doing my report on the cootie book.

"Look! It's the Poison Ivy Cootie Queen," Rose teased when I walked into class that morning. I ignored her.

"Ivy, why don't you start us off with the first book report?" asked Ms. Girth, before I even got to my desk.

That was weird. Usually we had flag first thing in the morning. Why did Ms. Girth have to pick today to be in such a hurry? I took my book to the front of the room and turned to face the class.

Wow! I couldn't believe my eyes! The whole class was in their underwear! (The Flower Girls all had flowers on theirs.) I shut my eyes tight and then looked again.

Whew! Everyone was back to normal. But now my mind had gone blank. I was frozen. A human Popsicle!

All of a sudden, I somehow unfroze and began talking. Fast!

"Mybookiscalled *BacteriaandYou*," I blurted. Who cared if I sounded like I was on fast-forward? I just wanted to get this over with!

In the middle of my report, Rose held up a big drawing of a bug wearing a crown. A cootie queen! The whole class began to giggle.

Next, the Flower Girls started scratching like they had poison ivy.

And Ms. Girth didn't do a thing about it! I glanced over at her. The teacher's

head was down on her desk, and she was making a soft buzzing sound. I looked more closely.

She was snoring! I had bored the teacher to sleep!

I stopped talking. What was the point of giving my report if Ms. Girth was sleeping?

But the minute I stopped talking, I began hiccuping. I hiccuped so loudly that the whole bed shook.

Wait a minute—*what bed?*

I sat up. I was in my room. In my bed! And it wasn't Friday. It was still just Tuesday night! My whole book report had been a nightmare.

Now I was more worried than ever.

I spotted my karate-class book on my bookshelf. Its neon-green cover seemed to glow. It was almost as if the book were trying to tell me something. . . .

Suddenly I had a great idea!

Chapter 7

The Nickname Note

It really was Friday this time, and I was ready.

But the minute I walked into class, Rose burst out laughing.

"Look!" she howled, pointing at me. "Poison Ivy is wearing pajamas!"

I looked down at my clothes. "These aren't pajamas. This is my karate gi."

Lily giggled and sang out, "Gee, it's her karate gi."

My karate suit fit right in at the dojo because everyone else wore one. But suddenly I felt stupid in it at school. Rose was right. It *did* look like pajamas.

After flag and math came book reports. Ms. Girth called on Violet to give hers first.

Violet went to the front of the class and held up her book. I waited for her to tell us the title and author, the way Ms. Girth had taught us. But she didn't. She just started talking about her book.

"There are lots of jump-rope songs in this book," Violet began. "I liked this book because there were lots of jump-rope songs."

"Didn't she just say that?" whispered Holly.

I nodded.

"There were nineteen—no, I mean twenty songs in this book," Violet went on. "I think." She paused and flipped through the pages, trying to count them.

Violet was fumbling around so much because she didn't have any notes! She hadn't written her report, so she was forgetting. A lot!

I doodled *Violet = Forgets-a-lot* on a scrap

of paper. Maybe I'd call her that from now on.

After Violet, it was Lily's turn. She went to the front of the room and held up her book. Then she mumbled something—the book's title?

I looked at Holly to see if she'd understood what Lily had said.

Holly raised and lowered her shoulders like she hadn't heard either. Lily continued giving her too-quiet book report.

"Talk louder," someone complained.

Lily turned pink.

"Shhh, class," said Ms. Girth. She leaned over and whispered something to Lily.

Lily nodded and went on with her report, but she kept on mumbling.

Maybe I should call her "Mumbles" from now on, I thought as Lily finished. I wrote *Lily = Mumbles* on my paper below *Violet = Forgets-a-lot.*

A couple of other kids gave reports, and then Ms. Girth called on Rose. I just knew her book report was going to be perfect!

Rose strutted to the front of the room like she was a princess. She held up a book with a ballerina on the cover.

Why hadn't I thought of giving my report on a ballerina book? That would have been a great choice. After all, who doesn't like ballerinas?

"My report is about this book," began Rose. "The title is . . . uh . . . *Ballerina Pinkies.* It was written by . . . uh . . . Emily Smith. There are five . . . uh . . . positions in ballet. This is first position." Rose put her book aside. She stuck her heels together, toes pointed outward. Her arms curved so that her fingertips met in front of her stomach.

"And this . . . uh . . . this is second," she continued as she showed us second position.

Rose sure was saying "uh" a lot. So far I had counted four "uh's" in her report. I made four tally marks on a sheet of paper. Rose kept talking, and I kept counting.

". . . And . . . uh . . . that's what it takes to become a ballerina," said Rose, finishing her report.

I added up the marks on my paper as Rose walked back to her seat. Twenty-six! Rose had said "uh" twenty-six times. That was *not* what I'd call perfect.

I wrote *Rose = Rose-uh* beneath the other nicknames. Now my note said:

Violet = Forgets-a-lot
Lily = Mumbles
Rose = Rose-uh

I nudged Holly and showed her.

"Perfect!" she said, giggling.

"Yeah," I whispered. "The Flower Girls should write a book called *How NOT to Give a Book Report.*"

We both grinned. I folded the note and tucked it under my karate belt. Just wait until lunch. Those Flower Girls were going to be sorry they'd ever picked on me!

Then came Ms. Girth's dreaded announcement.

"It's your turn, Ivy," she said.

Uh-oh!

Chapter 8

Karate Queen

I grabbed my book and my report and headed to the front of the room. When I reached Ms. Girth's desk, I turned around to face the class. I tried not to worry about what the other kids were thinking. I focused on what I wanted to tell them about my book.

"Ivy?" prompted Ms. Girth when the silence lengthened.

I took a deep breath. Then I began.

First I held up my book, moving it left to right so everyone could see the cover.

"My book is called *All About Karate.* It

was written by Benjamin Yeh." I spoke loudly but not too fast.

"Today I'm wearing my karate suit called a 'gi.' It's loose—sort of like *pajamas.*" (I darted a laser stare at Rose.) "Different colored karate belts show how much experience you have. At my school, white is the very beginner's belt. Next comes yellow, then green, blue, brown, and black. Black is for the most experienced.

"Karate teaches you to be courteous, respectful, and honest. In karate class, you have to want to learn and to always keep trying. Karate is for self-protection, but most of all karate is for fun."

I set my book and paper on the floor and kicked off my shoes.

"These are moves I learned in karate class and from this book," I said.

I bowed, then leaped into a karate stance.

"Kiaaaah!" I yelled, just like in karate class. I did chops. And punches.

The whole class was quiet. They were all watching and listening.

I bowed again after I had finished.

"Very nice, Ivy," said Ms. Girth, as I slipped my shoes back on. "Wearing your karate suit for your report was a great idea."

I was so happy, I felt as if I were wearing rocket-boosted, jet-propelled high-tops all the way back to my desk.

Now I knew the magic formula for performing in front of a crowd. Stay relaxed, be prepared, and don't worry about what the audience is thinking. My yellow-belt test was going to be a cinch after this. I might still be scared, but now I knew I'd be able to do it.

Chapter 9

No Cooties Allowed

At lunch I was a star. A regular Karate Queen. The other kids crowded around to ask me about karate.

I was dying to whip out my nickname note and read it to the Flower Girls.

Before I could, Rose pulled Holly aside. "We're going to let you in our club," she said.

"What about Ivy?" Holly asked.

"No cooties allowed," said Rose.

"Then thanks, but no thanks," Holly replied, scooting closer to me. "Besides, Ivy and I are starting our own club."

Rose sniffed. "What kind of club?"

Holly and I glanced at each other, panicking. We'd never decided on a club idea.

"A reading club," I blurted, from out of nowhere.

"Borrr-ing," sang Rose. "That's a dumb idea for a club."

"I like to read," said Brad.

"Me, too," chimed a few other kids.

"After our club reads a book, we can tell all the other kids if it's any good," Holly said. "And maybe we could all wear buttons with our club name."

"Can I be in the club?" asked Emily.

"I want to be in it, too!" cried Anna.

"What about me?" asked Brad. "Can I join? Or is it just for girls?"

Jay nudged Brad. "They'll make you read girl books," he warned.

"No, we'll vote on which books to read," I said. "Anyway, Holly and I like boy books, too."

"Maybe we could make up a skit about all of the books we've read and give it at the talent show," Holly said dreamily.

I could almost see a cloud of wacky club schemes begin to swirl around in Holly's brain.

Then she did the weirdest thing. Holly turned to the Flower Girls and said, "Why don't you join our club, too?"

Aaagh! I felt like thumping her. Was she crazy?

I aimed mind-control thought waves at Rose. *Please, please say no,* I thought.

"I might," said Violet.

"What!?" Rose demanded in surprise. "We already have a club!"

Violet shrugged. "I still want to be a Flower Girl, but it would be fun to be in a club that really *does* something."

"Yeah," Lily agreed. "And I have a good club name. How about the Book Buddies?"

"Or Bookworms," suggested Emily.

"What about Born 2 Read?" offered Brad.

"Wait! I've got a name for you," Rose butted in. "You could have your meetings at Ivy's house and call it the *COOTIES* club. That stands for *Come On Over To Ivy's Every Saturday*."

No one laughed. No one said anything. I flicked a corner of the nickname note hidden under my belt.

"We forgot to mention our biggest club rule," I said softly. "No name calling."

Splotches of red appeared on Rose's cheeks. She looked embarrassed! For once, Violet and Lily weren't siding with her. She looked like she wished she'd kept her mouth shut.

"Come on," she said to Violet and Lily. "Let's get out of here."

"Be there in a minute," said Lily.

"Me, too," said Violet. "I want to find out more about Ivy and Holly's club first."

Rose looked shocked but then quickly tried to cover it up. "Whatever . . . " she mumbled, shrugging like she didn't really care.

I watched Rose walk away all alone. Making her feel bad wasn't as much fun as I had thought it would be—even though she deserved it.

The bell rang, and we all headed inside.

I could hardly believe it was true. From now on, there would be no more Cootie Queen! No more Poison Ivy!

Lily and Violet couldn't call me names if they wanted to be in our club. And if Rose was the only one doing the name calling, she'd stop soon enough.

Of course, that also meant that I'd never get to call them Rose-uh, Forgets-a-lot, or Mumbles. But those secret nicknames would always help me remember that nobody's perfect.

Smiling, I skipped to catch up with Holly.

The cootie curse had finally ended!